Rainbow race

Follow the paths to see which unicorn finds the treasure.

Start →

← Start

Circle five red flowers.

Finish

Enchanted forest

Find the missing stickers, and then search for the things below.

How many of each animal can you find? Write the answers in the circles.

1 raccoon

3 owls

4

5 deer

How many acorns can you count? Write the answer.

Who doesn't belong?

3 🦄 unicorns

6 wands

5

11 🍄 toadstools

Unicorn nursery

Draw lines to match the baby unicorns to their dads.

Toadstool trot

Guide the unicorn across the meadow.
You can only step on the toadstools!

Princess picnic

Find and color...

- [x] ...a princess holding a pineapple.
- [ ] ...a dragon eating marshmallows.
- [x] ...a knight drinking juice.
- [x] ...a unicorn with a jar of jelly beans.
- [x] ...a fairy eating a cupcake.

Check the boxes as you find them.

Now add the missing stickers to finish!

9

Wonderful wands

Help the fairy find her missing wand.

How many wands can you count in each section?
Write the answers in the spaces below.

67

15

Answer: 13 star-shaped wands.

Answer: 16 heart-shaped wands.

Colorful carriage

Join the dots to finish the carriage.
Then sticker the passenger in the window.

Sea Safari

Use the clues to discover the unicorn's favorite underwater creature.

CLUE 1:
It is red.

CLUE 2:
It isn't swimming.

CLUE 3:
It has two pincers.

Answer: Lobster

Find the pairs of narwhals. Which one doesn't have a partner?

Sticker what's hiding in the seaweed.

13

Rainbow rows

Circle the one that is different on each row.

Party time!

Use color and stickers to make the cakes match.

How many balloons
can you count?
Write the answer. ....

Winter wonderland

Find the missing stickers to finish the ice castle.

Follow the lines to see who wins the race.

1ST

3RD

2ND

17

Swirly style

Doodle swirls and patterns on the unicorn
to give her a beautiful makeover.

CRAYON

CRAYON

CRAYON

CRAYON

CRAYON

Sticker flower accessories
in her mane.

Gorgeous Jewels

Unscramble the letters to reveal the jewels.
Then put them in the crossword.

1 LSIVRE
S_LVE_

2 MBARE
A_BER

3 SAHIPEPR
SAP_HI_E

4 UBRY
_UBY

5 DMAONDI
DIA_O_D

6 EPARL
P_ARL

7 DOLG
G_LD

Which jewel is hiding in the green gems?

19

Magic mountains

Find the missing stickers to finish the scene.

How many of each animal can you find?
Write the answers in the circles.

1 .... bear

.... moose

.... eagles

.... chicks

.... squirrels

.... unicorns

.... foxes

.... goats

21

Movie Night

Trace the letters to reveal what movie
the unicorns are watching.

unicorn

squad

How many boxes of popcorn
can you count? Write the answer.

Cool campsite

Draw another tent for the unicorns.
Use the grid to guide you.

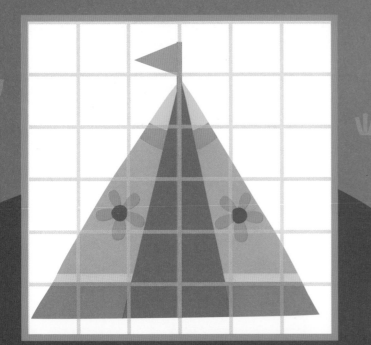

Find the missing stickers to see who is singing by the campfire.

Rainbow rush

Use the press-out counters and cards at the back of the book to play the game.

Start

Grant a wish!
Move ahead 1.

Lose your wand.
Go back 2.

Stop for a tea party.
Miss a turn.

Slide down a rainbow.
Move ahead 3.

Best friends forever!
Join any player's counter
on the board.

Watch the sunset.
Go back 1.

Finish

25

Super skate

Color the picture.

Find and circle five rainbows.

At the Beach

Sticker the empty boxes to fill the grid. There should only be one of each image in any column or row.

Secret garden

Guide the unicorn across the pond.
Use the key to guide you.

KEY:

Circle five things you need to make flowers grow.

milk CHOCO

Which row of flowers matches the silhouette? Write the answer.

· · · · · · · · · ·

A

B

C

Answer: C

Beautiful butterflies

Are there more pink butterflies or blue butterflies?

☐ pink   ☐ blue

Trace the flight paths of the butterflies.

30

Sticker and color to finish the butterfly's wings.

Fairy Food

Find the missing stickers to help the fairies
feed the hungry unicorns!

End of the rainbow

Find the words in the grid below.
Words can go across or down.

fairy

jewels

magic

rainbow

unicorn

wand

f	h	r	w	n	c	x	s	o	y	v	b
a	e	j	e	w	e	l	s	r	u	j	s
i	v	q	z	r	t	i	h	n	r	m	m
r	x	j	b	e	c	t	u	m	u	i	a
y	r	q	b	u	j	s	n	l	o	p	g
s	d	f	e	s	a	w	i	n	g	t	i
r	e	m	h	j	r	x	c	c	b	j	c
b	q	r	a	i	n	b	o	w	l	m	n
e	r	k	u	i	b	v	r	u	h	y	t
w	q	f	r	i	b	e	n	x	t	v	c
t	y	n	v	l	u	i	m	q	b	y	s
v	e	h	b	w	n	c	s	w	a	n	d

Stardust skies

Join the dots to finish the constellations.

LEO

HERCULES

THE BIG DIPPER

CASSIOPEIA

Find the missing stickers
to finish the picture.

Can you find five things that
don't belong in the night sky?

Make a wish

Unicorns grant wishes.
Draw what you would wish for here!

Pretty palace

Can you find all the things below?
Check the boxes as you find them.

Ahoy, Matey!

Guide the unicorn pirate ship across the rainbow seas.
Look out for rocks!

Start

How many mermaids can
you count? Write the answer. ....

Finish

Find and circle six turtles.

Balloon ride

Sticker and color to finish the picture.

40

Sports day

Use the key to solve the sums.
Write the totals in the circles at the end.

$\bowtie$ = 1   🏀 = 3   🍾 = 2

The unicorn
with the most points
wins the race!

Tasty treats

Circle the cupcake that matches the sum.

+ + + =

How many flavors of ice-cream sundae can you count?

Write the answer.

....

Doodle delicious toppings on the donuts.

Which one doesn't belong?

Find and circle two cookies that match.

43

Sweet sleepover

Color the picture.
Use the dots to guide you.

Rainbow rush game

How to play:

1. Choose one counter each and place it on the Start space.

2. Shuffle the cards and place them facedown.

3. Take turns picking the top card from the pile to find out what to do. Return each card to the bottom of the pile after using it.

4. The winner is the first one to cross the finish line.

This is a game for 2 to 4 players. Use these two pages of press-out pieces with the game on pages 24-25.

Miss a turn.

Throw a surprise party for Squirrel.

Move ahead 1.

Find a magic acorn.

Move ahead 2.

Help a friend.

Move ahead 2.

Discover a shortcut.

Miss a turn.

Stop to fly with the birds.

Go back 2.

Take a wrong turn.

cards

counters

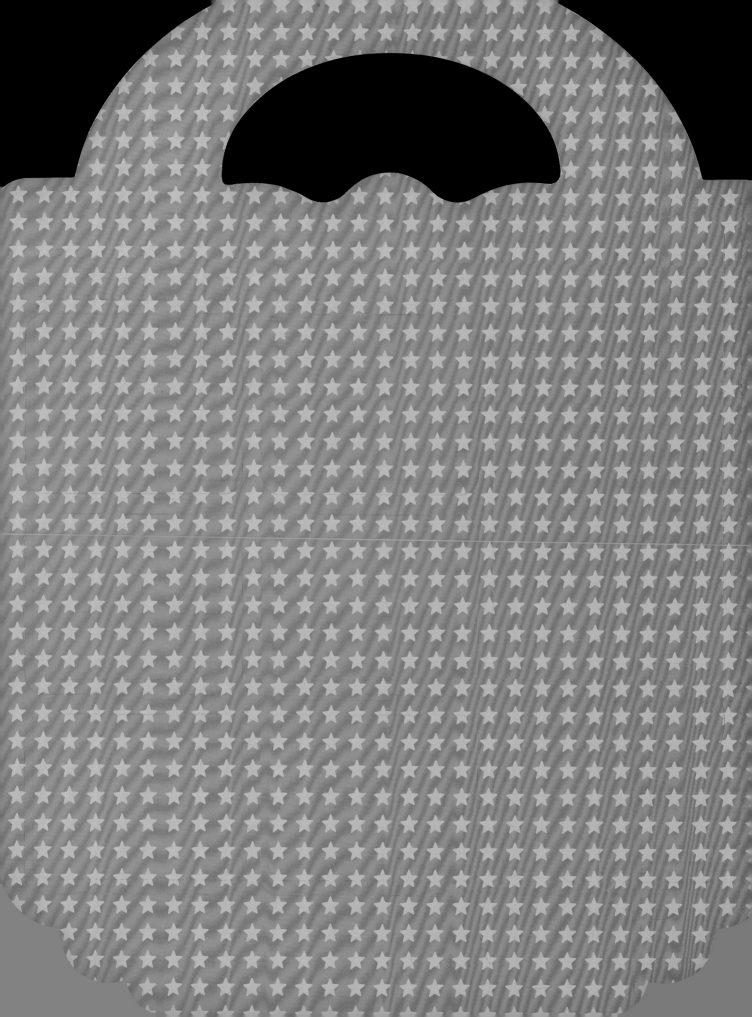

Rainbow rush game

Press out these cards for the game.

Follow a shooting star. Move ahead 3.

Skip over stepping-stones. Move ahead 1.

Fairy dust shower! Move ahead 2.

Stop to make a hot drink. Miss a turn.

See the sunrise. Move ahead 1.

Sing with the princess. Go back 1.

Choose any player on the board to move back 3 spaces.

Get lost in Lollipop Woods. Go back 2.

Hitch a ride with a fairy. Move ahead 3.

Unicorn palace

1. Press out the palace and unicorn pieces.

2. Open the slots on the palace and fold along the creases. Push it forward to make it 3-D.

3. Use the unicorns to bring the palace to life.

Unicorn mask

Press out the unicorn mask
and the eye holes. Then ask an
adult to help you thread some
ribbon through the holes and
tie it around your head.

Brilliant bookmarks

Press out the bookmarks and use them to mark the most fun activities in this book!

Pretty puzzle

Press out the puzzle pieces and mix them up.
Now put them back together to make this picture.

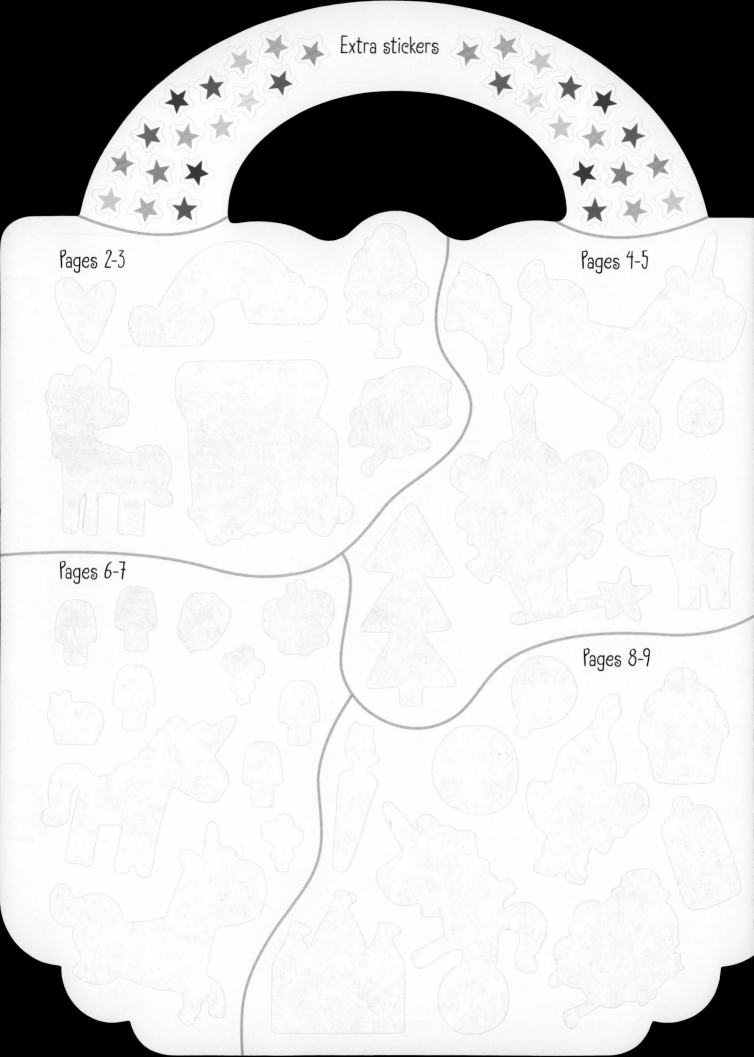

Extra stickers

Pages 2-3

Pages 4-5

Pages 6-7

Pages 8-9

Extra stickers

Pages 28-29

Pages 30-31

Page 32

Extra stickers

Extra stickers

Page 33

Page 35

Page 37

Pages 40-41

Pages 38-39

Page 42

Extra stickers

Page 42 cont'd

Page 43

Extra stickers

Extra stickers